D1495792

Widdermaker

by Pattie Schnetzler • **pictures by Rick Sealock**

Carolrhoda Books, Inc./Minneapolis

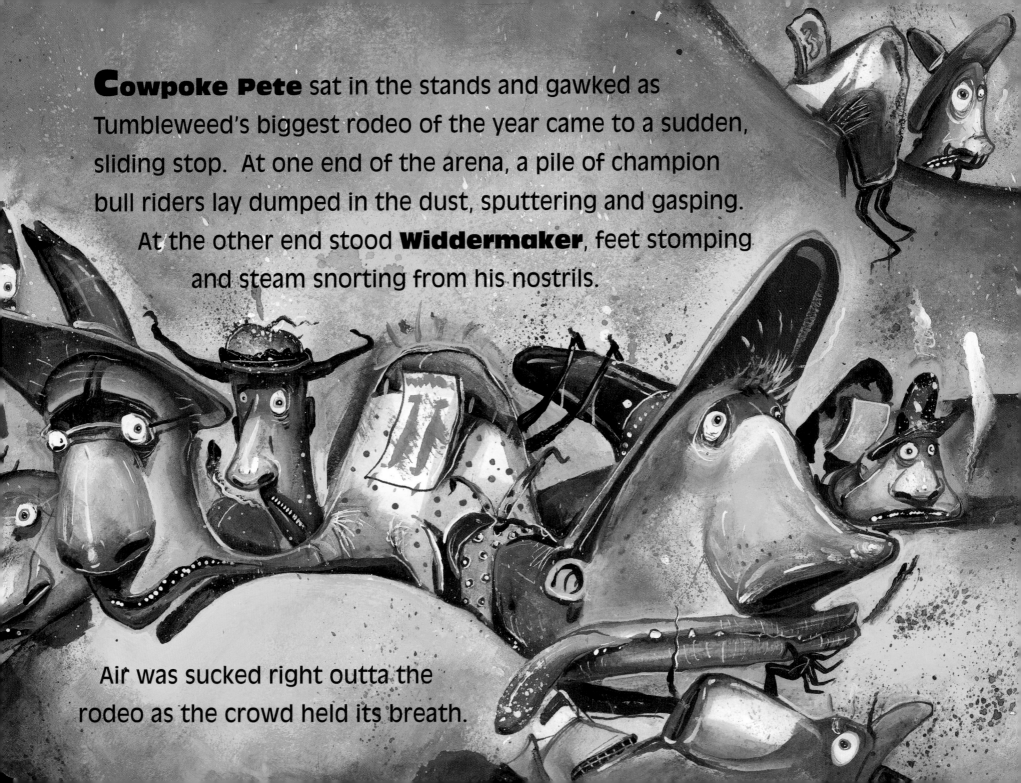

Cowpoke Pete sat in the stands and gawked as Tumbleweed's biggest rodeo of the year came to a sudden, sliding stop. At one end of the arena, a pile of champion bull riders lay dumped in the dust, sputtering and gasping. At the other end stood **Widdermaker**, feet stomping and steam snorting from his nostrils.

Air was sucked right outta the rodeo as the crowd held its breath.

Widdermaker bellowed. Then he reached around and bit a snitch-a-hair outta his hide. It was that ornery bull's way of keeping score: **Widdermaker—12, Cowboys—0.**

Cowpoke Pete shifted. "Tarnation," he spat. "Varmints is varmints. And cowpokes is cowpokes. And varmints don't beat cowpokes."

Pete stood up to face the challenge, just as Widdermaker busted out of the arena and hightailed it through the town of Tumbleweed, crashing and smashing everything in his path.

"That bull's plumb loco,"
yelled a cowboy.
   "If he's not roped, he's gonna
destroy the entire West," shouted
Cowpoke Pete. "Loco or not,
I aim to tame 'im."

Pete strode toward the corral to have a cowpoke-to-cowpony talk with **Desert Rose**. Now, Rose wasn't your ordinary cowpony. She was the fastest pony west of the Mississippi, and she was painted with the colors of the setting sun.

"He's big and he's mean," whinnied Pete.

Desert Rose tossed her head and swished her tail.

"Let's go git 'im!" Pete swung into the saddle and headed after the meanest low-downest bull the West had ever seen.

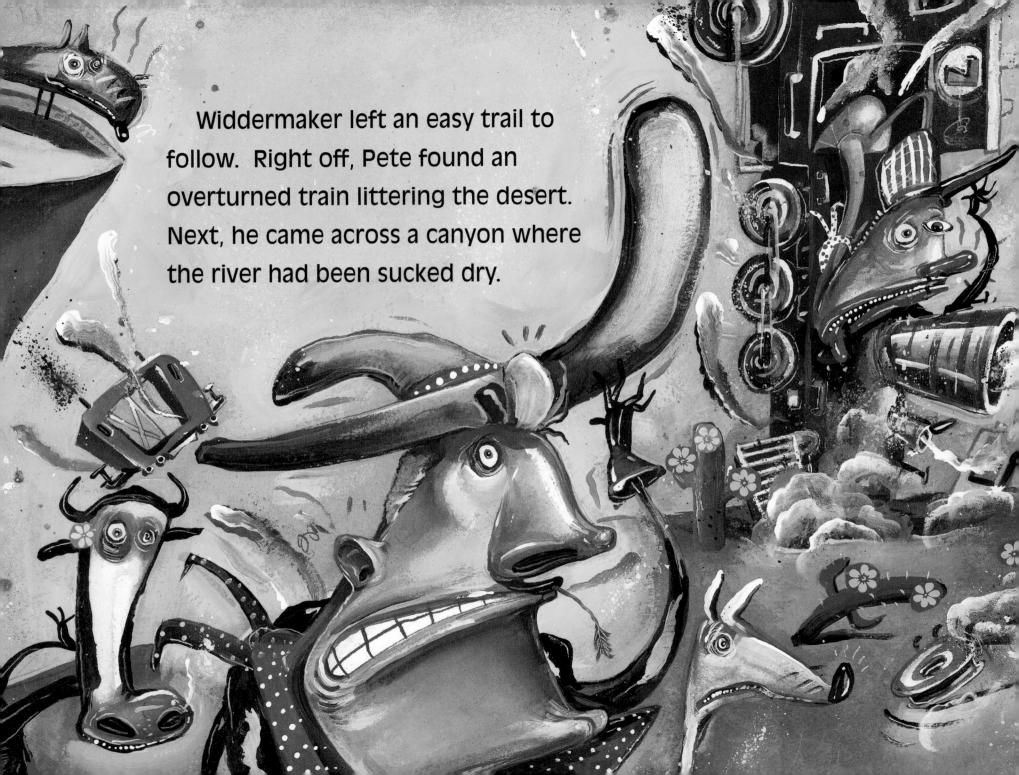

Widdermaker left an easy trail to follow. Right off, Pete found an overturned train littering the desert. Next, he came across a canyon where the river had been sucked dry.

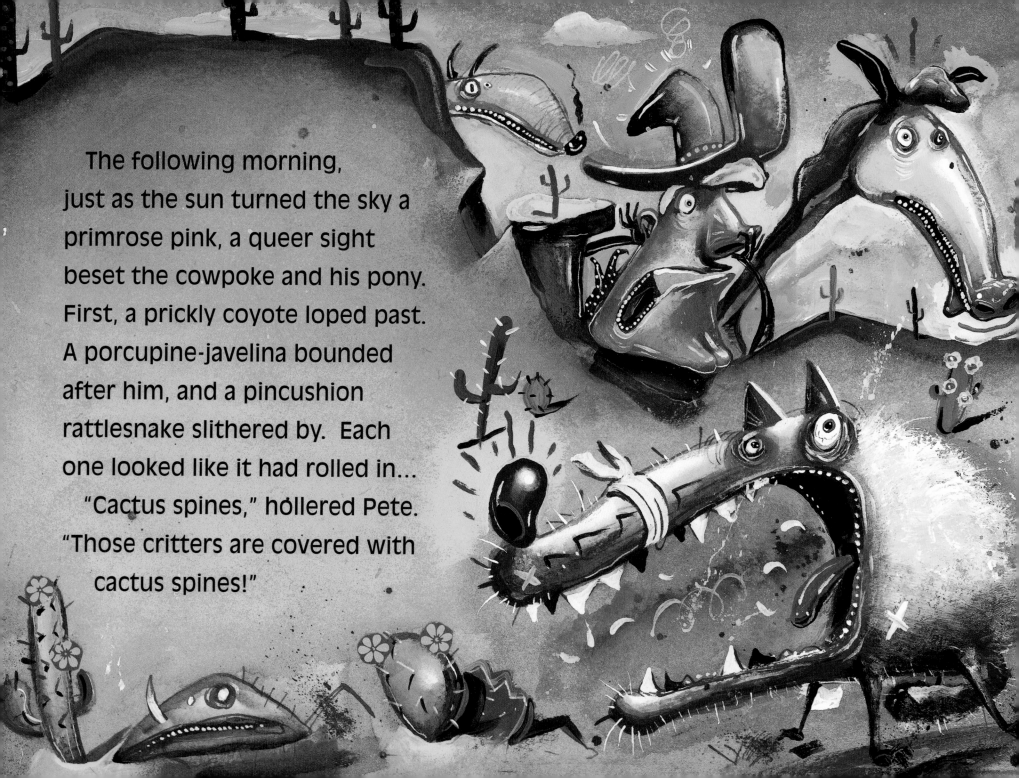

The following morning, just as the sun turned the sky a primrose pink, a queer sight beset the cowpoke and his pony. First, a prickly coyote loped past. A porcupine-javelina bounded after him, and a pincushion rattlesnake slithered by. Each one looked like it had rolled in...

"Cactus spines," hollered Pete. "Those critters are covered with cactus spines!"

Then, across the desert,
they spied Widdermaker.

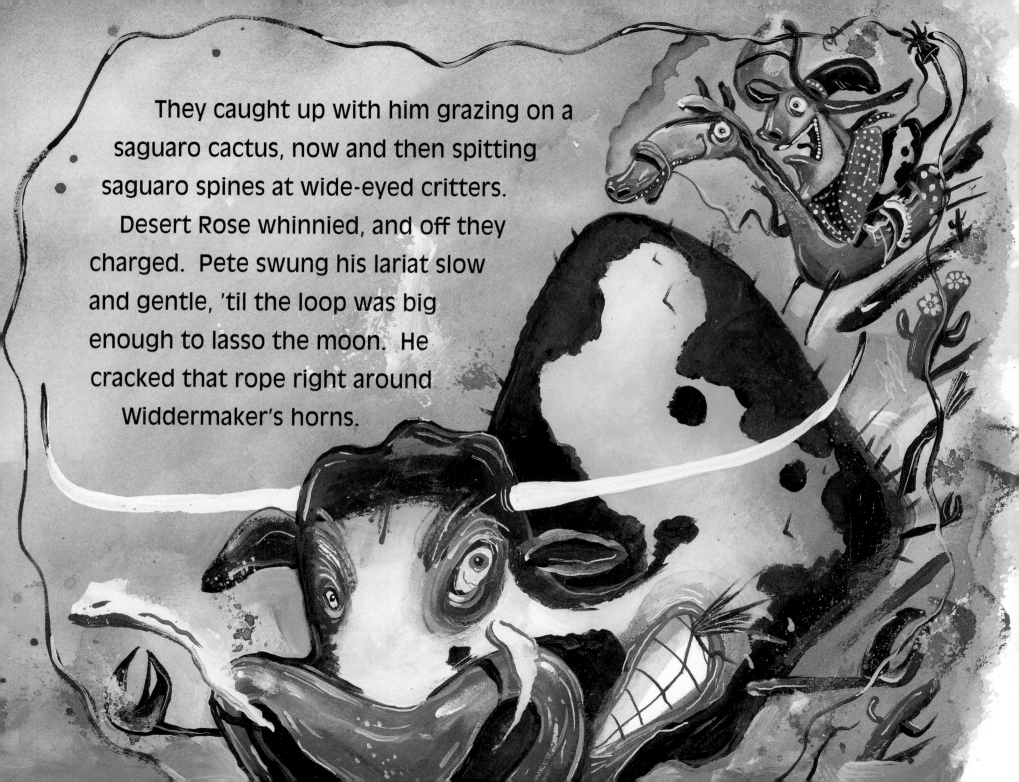

They caught up with him grazing on a saguaro cactus, now and then spitting saguaro spines at wide-eyed critters. Desert Rose whinnied, and off they charged. Pete swung his lariat slow and gentle, 'til the loop was big enough to lasso the moon. He cracked that rope right around Widdermaker's horns.

Desert Rose dug in with her haunches as Pete wrapped the lariat tight around his saddle horn. Widdermaker came up short.

Wild-eyed, the bull jerked and slobbered. Tail twitching, he snorted and kicked up the desert into a cyclone of dust, cactus, and critters. Widdermaker bellowed so loud that the earth and the sky shuddered, but that didn't scare Desert Rose. She played the lariat and pulled Widdermaker outta that cyclone. Then the rope went limp.

Suddenly, there stood Widdermaker eyeball to eyeball with Pete and Rose. The bull gave a snort and took off like a runaway train, dragging his cargo behind him.

They flew behind that bull, lost in a blur of colors. Pete grinned like a jacky-lantern. "Yippee, yippee, yahoo! What a ride!"

"Tarnation, Rose," said Pete, when they finally slowed down. "You're as white as a newborn calf." Then Pete looked behind him, and a startling sight stirred his heart.

"Lookit, Rose! The desert is painted with your colors." He smiled, then peered back around at the bull, who was fast recovering his breath.

Widdermaker was mad!

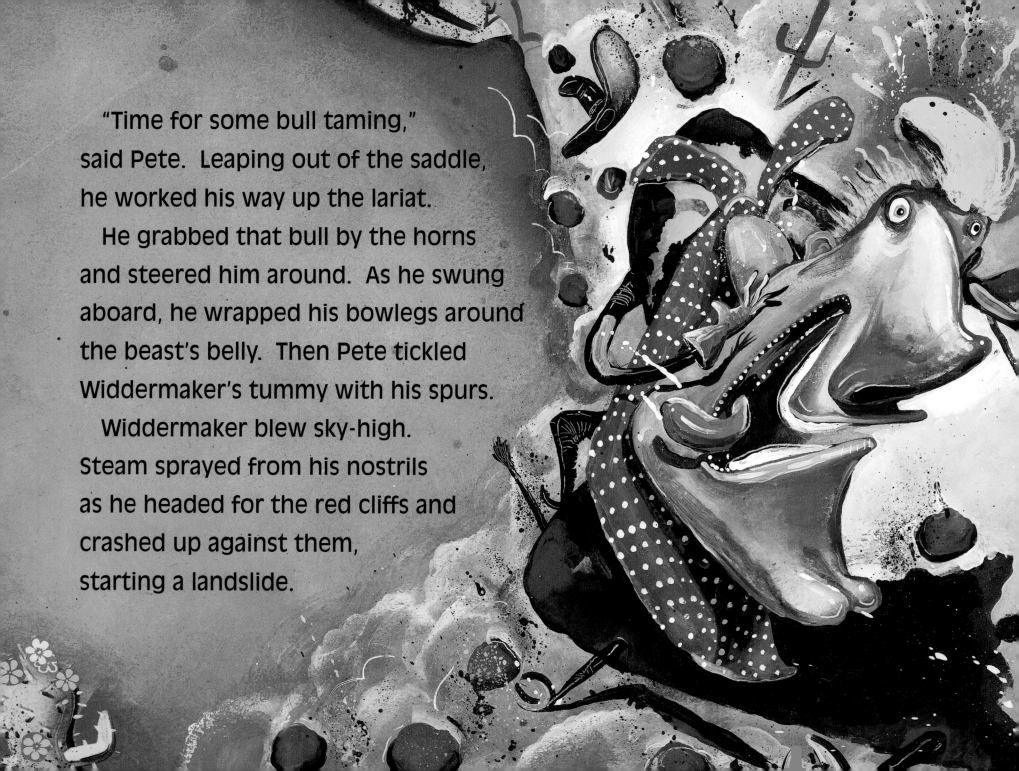

"Time for some bull taming,"
said Pete. Leaping out of the saddle,
he worked his way up the lariat.
   He grabbed that bull by the horns
and steered him around. As he swung
aboard, he wrapped his bowlegs around
the beast's belly. Then Pete tickled
Widdermaker's tummy with his spurs.
   Widdermaker blew sky-high.
Steam sprayed from his nostrils
as he headed for the red cliffs and
crashed up against them,
starting a landslide.

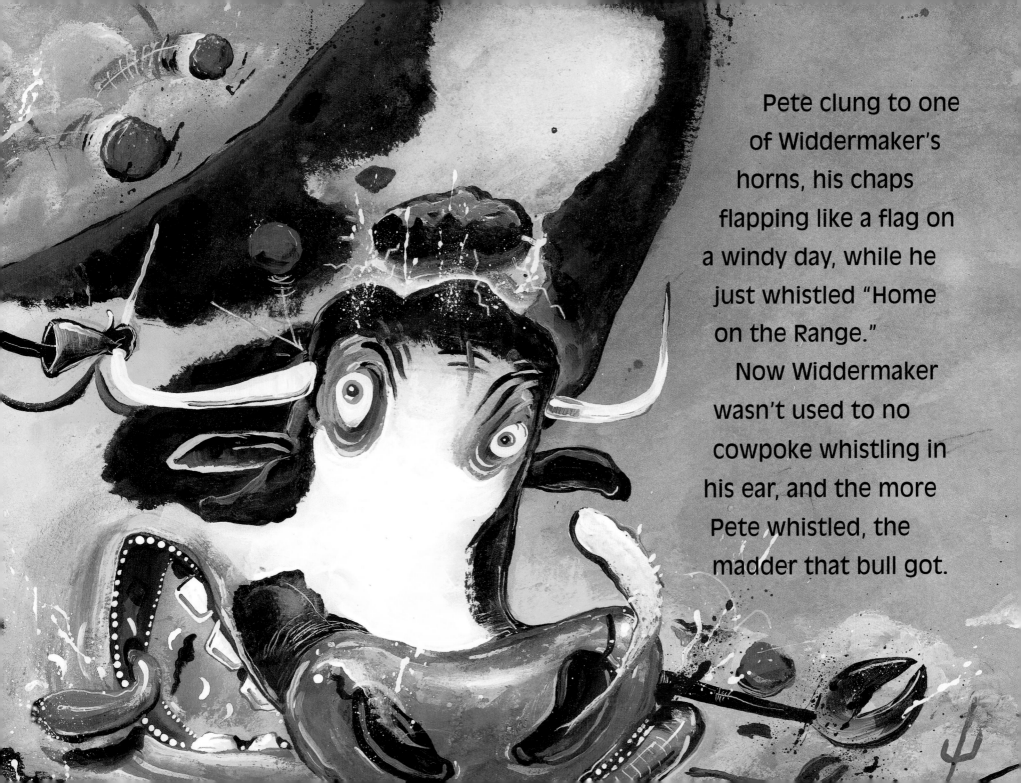

Pete clung to one of Widdermaker's horns, his chaps flapping like a flag on a windy day, while he just whistled "Home on the Range."

Now Widdermaker wasn't used to no cowpoke whistling in his ear, and the more Pete whistled, the madder that bull got.

"Cowpokes is cowpokes," hollered Pete as he took a snitch-a-hair out of Widdermaker's hide. "And varmints is varmints." He took another snitch. "And varmints don't beat cowpokes."

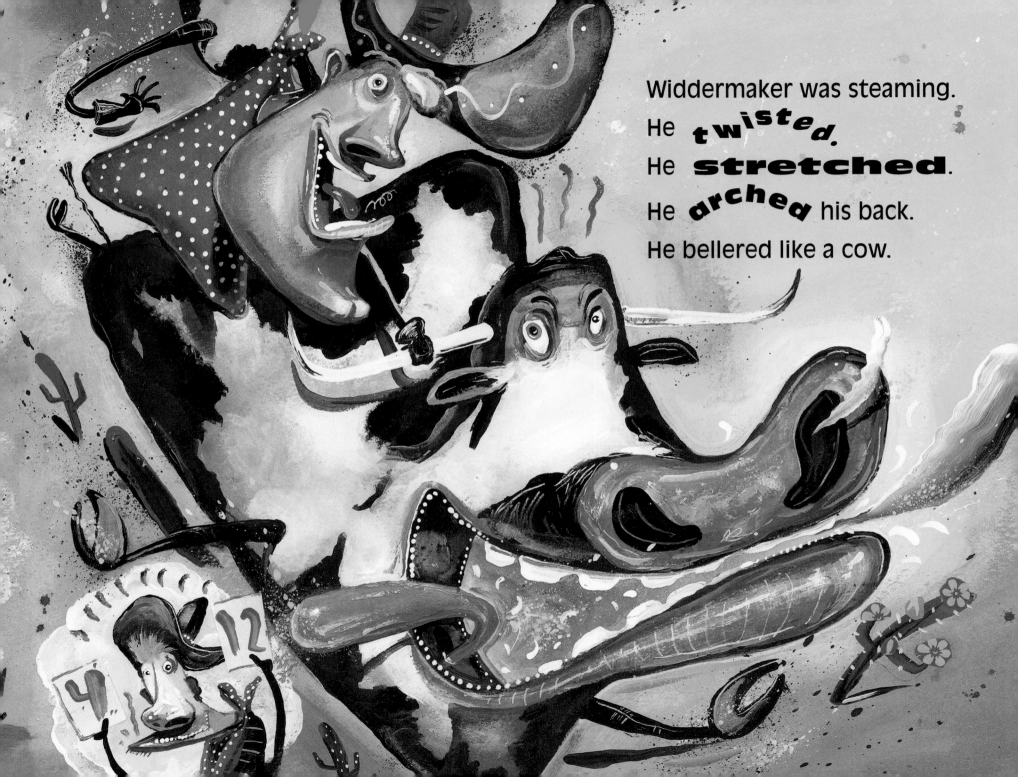

Widdermaker was steaming.
He **twisted**.
He **stretched**.
He **arched** his back.
He bellered like a cow.

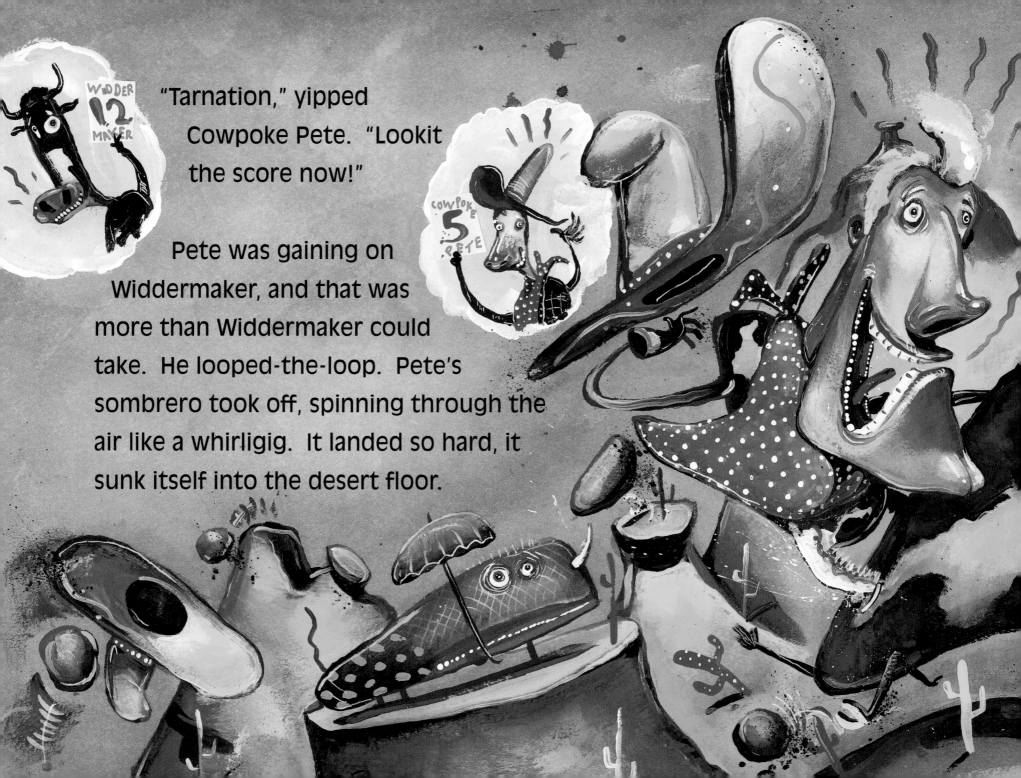

"Tarnation," yipped Cowpoke Pete. "Lookit the score now!"

Pete was gaining on Widdermaker, and that was more than Widdermaker could take. He looped-the-loop. Pete's sombrero took off, spinning through the air like a whirligig. It landed so hard, it sunk itself into the desert floor.

Still hanging on, Pete yelled,
"Tarnation, that was the best gol-durn
Mexican Hat I ever had."

Widdermaker charged
through the red rock
valley like a steam engine
blowing its stack. Pete
hung on, whistlin'
through his teeth, all the
while keeping score.

Suddenly, the bull stopped, and Pete heard the rumble of loud thunder. He looked up, expecting to see black clouds. But the wide-open sky stretched bold and blue as far as the eye could see.

That's when Pete noticed that Widdermaker was snoring like a rumblin' thundercloud.

"Well, I'll be," Pete said to Rose. "Looks like ol' Widdermaker's outta gas."

Pete checked the score. "There ya have it,"
he grinned. He ringed the bull's nose.
"Varmint," he said, "you've been tamed."
Widdermaker grinned
sheepishly, as the setting sun
smiled and a pink glow washed
the red rock valley.

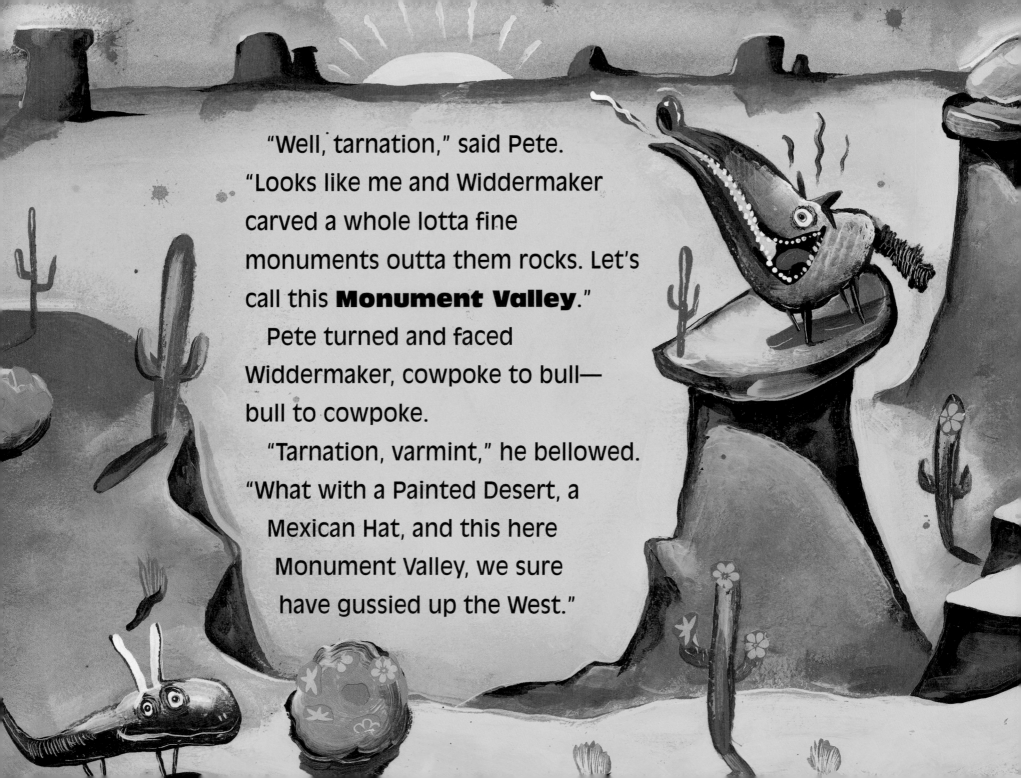

"Well, tarnation," said Pete. "Looks like me and Widdermaker carved a whole lotta fine monuments outta them rocks. Let's call this **Monument Valley**."

Pete turned and faced Widdermaker, cowpoke to bull— bull to cowpoke.

"Tarnation, varmint," he bellowed. "What with a Painted Desert, a Mexican Hat, and this here Monument Valley, we sure have gussied up the West."

That night, Cowpoke Pete, Desert Rose, and Widdermaker rode into Tumbleweed for a celebration. The cowboys were so impressed, they gave Pete a big silver belt buckle that read, "World Champion Bull Tamer." Pete and Rose felt mighty proud.

Not long after that, Pete, Desert Rose, and Widdermaker decided that gussying up the West was the trail they were called upon to follow.

"There's this little ol' canyon out there," Pete told the cowboys on his way out of Tumbleweed.

"Me, Desert Rose, and Widdermaker aim to make it Grand."

For my daughter, Kailee, and her gift of Desert Rose,
the purtiest horse in the West —P. S.

For my little buckaroos, Christina, Pig, Nox,
and the El Freako Kid —R. S.

Carolrhoda Books, Inc.
A division of Lerner Publishing Group
241 First Avenue North
Minneapolis, MN 55401 U.S.A.

Website address: www.lernerbooks.com

Library of Congress Cataloging-in-Publication Data

Schnetzler, Pattie L., 1952–
    Widdermaker / by Pattie Schnetzler ; Illustrations by Rick Sealock.
      p.   cm.
    Summary: The efforts of Cowpoke Pete and his pony, Desert Rose, to tame
Widdermaker, the meanest, low-downest bull the West had ever seen, have
unexpected and very pleasant results.
    ISBN: 0–87614–647–7 (lib. bdg. : alk. paper)
    [1. Cowboys—Fiction. 2. Bulls—Fiction. 3. Horses—Fiction. 4. West (U.S.)—
Fiction. 5. Tall tales. 6. Humorous stories.] I. Sealock, Rick, ill. II. Title.
PZ7.S36433 Wi 2002
[Fic]—dc21   2001006136

Manufactured in the United States of America
1 2 3 4 5 6 – JR – 07 06 05 04 03 02

**You can find the places Widdermaker
gussied up in Utah and Arizona.**